THE GREY MAN

Andy McNab

LARGE PRINT

First published in 2006 by
Corgi
This Large Print edition published
2006 by BBC Audiobooks by
arrangement with
Trandworld Publishers Ltd

ISBN 1 4056 2196 6
ISBN 13: 978 1 405 62196 0

Quick Reads™ used under licence

British Library Cataloguing in Publication Data available

Printed and bound in Great Britain by the MPG Books Group

CHAPTER ONE

The Bank, Ipswich
Friday, 3 February 2006, 4.51 p.m.

From his desk Kevin looked through the glass security screen at the three men in long raincoats about to rob the bank. He could see the shapes of their sawn-off shotguns bulging out from under their coats. His heart started to beat faster, almost jumping out of his chest. Why hadn't anyone else noticed?

One robber stood at the credit point. He was going to make sure no one got in or out of the bank's main door once the robbery went down. Another was in the queue for Gary, the only clerk on duty at that time in the afternoon. He would hand a note to Gary that read, 'Put both hands where I can see them and call the manager. If not, you all die.' The

1

third man, the leader, was reading a poster about bank loans. He was close to the security door that led to the staff side of the screen.

Kevin knew what would happen. Gary would call the manager and he would be told to open the security door. The gang leader would burst in and grab the cash while the other two controlled the customers and staff.

The plan was simple, quick and violent. Anyone in their way would get the good news from the business end of the shotguns. They must be on drugs because Kevin couldn't understand why they weren't worried about the cameras, which would already have taped enough film for the police to ID them. But Kevin didn't have time to think about that now. He had to take action. He reached under his desk and felt for the alarm that would alert the local police station.

His hand shook a little as it

2

hovered near the button. From his office he watched Gary say goodbye to Mr Field and start talking to another customer. The robber was next in line.

The second robber, standing at the credit point, headed for the main door. The leader undid his raincoat, ready to draw down his gun before he burst through the security door. Kevin's throat was dry as he moved his hand away from the alarm button. It was too late. The police wouldn't get there in time. Customers' lives were in danger and someone had to save them.

That someone had to be Kevin. Only he could see what was about to happen. He couldn't shout and raise the alarm. The gang might panic and try to shoot their way out. The only way to stop the robbery was to jump the leader before he passed the note to Gary. If Kevin had the leader's gun, he could arrest the robbers himself. If the other two drew down

3

their weapons to take him on, he would just have to shoot it out with them. He felt a little excited at the prospect.

Gary had nearly finished with his customer. The robber was next. Now wasn't the time for thinking. It was the time for doing. Kevin took a deep breath and prepared to take down the three-man crew.

CHAPTER TWO

'Dodds! Wake up. If you stopped dreaming, you might get some work done! You're the laziest man I've ever met.' Albert Symington, the bank manager, was clearly in another bad mood. 'Remember, Dodds, I want that report in first thing on Monday morning.'

Kevin watched Gary greet the robber. Well, actually, it was Greg Jameson who ran the local heel bar.

In fact, none of the three robbers were really robbers. And it wasn't only the robbers who were wearing raincoats. Every customer had one on today because it was raining. It had been all day. But that didn't worry Kevin. He liked to day-dream, and play 'what if'. He was bored out of his mind at work. He wanted a bit of excitement.

Symington was still yelling at him but Kevin just smiled. He always smiled when his boss yelled. 'The report? I've already done it, Mr Symington.' He pulled it, in its new blue folder, from his desk drawer. 'I finished it today, during lunch.'

'About bloody time too.' Symington snatched it out of Kevin's hand and stormed off to find another victim.

It was a shame his day-dream had been ruined just before the good bit. Kevin wouldn't play action hero today. Never mind, there was always tomorrow. No doubt he would finish his work early then too.

Kevin got up and went over to Gary, who was counting a wad of twenties. 'Got the stapler?'

Gary nodded at it. 'He does like having a go at you, doesn't he, Kev?' He kept his voice down. Nothing wrong with Symington's hearing.

Kevin shrugged as he watched Gary's fingers flick through the notes. 'Yep, but what's new?' He picked up the stapler. Symington didn't only shout at Kevin, he shouted at all four of the staff for being too slow or lazy. It was really Symington who was slow and lazy. He was the only one not doing his job properly. Unless, of course, he was meant to go around and shout at people all day.

Gary slipped a paper band round a thousand pounds' worth of twenties, then started on another wad. He was the only one of them who could count and talk at the same time. 'Don't know why the little shit doesn't leave you alone. You always get the worst of it, and you're doing his job as well as your own.'

Gary didn't even look at the notes as he counted them. Kevin thought he would be better suited to dealing cards in Las Vegas than working in a bank.

'I reckon he's scared you're going to take his job, mate.' Gary often said exactly what Kevin was thinking.

Kevin had worked in this poxy bank for nine years now. Since leaving college, he had slogged his way up the ladder from trainee to deputy manager, and what thanks did he get? He'd saved Symington's arse hundreds of times, but all he ever got was abuse. Symington was great at sucking up to Head Office, but he was crap at running a bank. Even a bank as small as this one. He made *The Office*'s David Brent look like Richard Branson. But instead of answering Symington back, and telling him how crap he was, Kevin kept quiet. For nine years he had held his tongue and covered up Symington's mistakes. He had done it so often, that it had become the norm.

He felt he had no other option. Head Office was always looking to cut costs. If they decided to close a branch, Middle Street, Ipswich, would be the one. There were two larger banks in the city centre, and theirs didn't rake in millions. It also looked old-fashioned. It hadn't had a refit in twenty years and soon it would need money spending on it. But, much as he hated his job, Kevin didn't want the bank to close. He needed his wage, and he didn't want to be sent to a branch on the other side of the country. His wife Linda wanted to stay in Ipswich to be close to her mum, whose health was poor. There never seemed to be any jobs going at the other banks in town, and Ipswich wasn't full of good jobs for guys like him. So he had to stick with what he'd got. So what if he had to save his boss now and then? He liked his three workmates and one day Symington would retire. Then maybe The Bank, Middle Street, Ipswich, would be the hot ticket in town. That was why good old Kevin just smiled and got on with his work when Symington shouted at him. But it was harder and harder to force that smile.

'I know I should tell him where to go, Gary, but I want next Friday off, remember?'

'Yeah, right.' Gary wasn't fooled. They both knew Kevin would never step out of line. 'Planning anything special for the big day?'

'Not really. It's just nice to have the time together. Linda loves that Italian in Morton Street. We go there every year.'

'Dodds!' Symington was back. 'If you're not day-dreaming, you're chatting. Get those safe-deposit records updated before you go home. And make me a coffee while you're at it, will you?'

Symington went back to his office and slumped into his leather chair. Even from where he was standing, Kevin could see sweat dripping on to his mad-Major moustache.

CHAPTER THREE

Kevin went to the staff kitchen and filled the kettle. He had already updated those records, so he didn't have any work to do. He liked looking after the safe-deposit boxes down in the basement. He got to see all sorts of wonderful things going into them. He had to step aside while a customer placed their items in their box, but sometimes they asked for help, or they made a show of loading the box with jewellery or money. Often they wanted Kevin to look. Last week, old George Rowlands

10

had brought in a skull. His hands were shaking so much with some illness that he couldn't open his box, so Kevin had had to help him.

Kevin had wondered why George might have made that deposit. He wasn't what you would call a nice man to deal with, so Kevin had come up with some not very nice theories. He had decided that George had murdered his wife, then dug up what was left of her from under the patio. His two sons were planning to build him a lean-to so old George was bringing in her body piece by piece before they started. His deposit box was one of the larger ones. That was because it contained a black box, about the size of a briefcase, in which George kept nearly £100,000 in fifty-pound notes.

George had boasted to Kevin about his cash when he came into the bank one afternoon to pay some money into his current account. He always came in at the same time each month and paid in the same amount—two hundred pounds. He had had quite a lot to drink that day and couldn't stop himself spilling the beans.

Apparently he had cheated the VAT man when he had had his own building firm, and this little nest egg was the result. He had to put it in a deposit box, he said, because if it ever got nicked he wouldn't be able to report it. He was proud to say that he'd never looked inside the money box from the day he had put in the cash. He'd never touched it, and never would. He had more than enough money going into his current account to last him the rest of his life. Not even his wife and two sons knew about the secret stash.

That seemed a shame to Kevin, because George's wife had died of cancer two years ago. Maybe she could have spent it on better care. He had gone to school with George's two sons and had kept in touch with them over the years. He knew that they helped out their dad with any spare cash they had. He wondered if that was where the two hundred pounds came from each month.

It didn't seem right to Kevin that stingy George took money from his kids and never let on that he had all that cash of his own. He was keeping it for a rainy day, he said. And he wasn't going to let anyone else have a penny of it. Certainly not those useless sons of his—the wasters. Kevin knew it was none of his business what George did with his money. His job was to open the first lock on the deposit box for George and that was it.

Kevin took the lid off the jumbo-sized Nescafé jar that was sitting on the table.

When Symington had lost his diary last year, the names of customers who had deposit boxes had been written on the back page. Kevin had been saying for months that they should put the records on to the computer, and so had Head Office, but Symington refused. He didn't do computers, he said.

The day the diary got lost, Kevin had never seen Symington in such a state. He ran round the office like a headless chicken, checking every desk, every filing cabinet, every wastepaper bin. He twirled his moustache, as he always did when he was upset. Kevin would have found it very funny if the bank hadn't been expecting a visit from Head Office that day. They had phoned in the morning to say they were coming down later for a safe-deposit system inspection. Symington was likely to lose his job because the records weren't on the computer.

When the man from Head Office came in, Kevin had lied. He said the computer was down. He had saved Symington's arse again and maybe all of their jobs too. Since then, Kevin had pieced together which deposit

14

box belonged to whom and finally put everyone's name on the computer. Symington had never thanked him. Just like he wouldn't on Monday when Kevin sent off the monthly report as if Symington had done it himself.

Kevin made his boss a cup of coffee. He'd ask for next Friday off now. He couldn't wait to see the smile on Linda's face when he told her he'd swung a long weekend for their wedding anniversary.

He headed for Symington's office, careful not to spill the brew on the carpet. He felt himself tense up. He knew it was stupid to be nervous of the old git, but he couldn't help it. 'Come on, Kevin,' he muttered. 'Think tough. Think mean. Think killer shark. You can do it.' He started to hum the *Jaws* tune. He felt tough. He felt mean. He was that killer shark.

'Mr Symington, I wonder if—'

The coffee leaped out of Kevin's

hands and splashed over Symington's neat pin-striped suit. Symington jumped out of his chair and pulled at his shirt to keep the hot liquid off his skin. 'Can't you even walk past a wastepaper basket?' he roared

'So sorry, Mr Symington. I didn't see—'

'You clumsy oaf. You'll get the dry-cleaning bill on Monday.'

'I'm sorry, I didn't see the bin and I—'

'What is it you want anyway?'

Now Kevin felt less like a killer shark and more like a beached whale. 'Nothing,' he muttered. 'Can't remember.' He stumbled out of Symington's office. At least it was the end of the week and he wouldn't have to see the man until Monday. Maybe he would have calmed down by then and Kevin could have another shot at asking him for next Friday off.

CHAPTER FOUR

Kevin sat on the top deck of the bus, with his briefcase on his lap. He normally sat downstairs because he hadn't far to go. Today he had helped an old lady and she wouldn't stop thanking him so he had come upstairs to escape. He could see the whole of the high street through the rain-stripped windows. Lots of men with briefcases and umbrellas struggled up the hill to the car park. Office girls huddled in the doorway of Boots, smoking.

A woman with a pram tucked a new mop under one arm as she pushed with the other hand. Then she lost her grip on the pram, which started to roll down the hill. She dropped the mop and grabbed the pram. The baby was safe. For a moment, Kevin saw himself as Superman, in red cape and blue tights, smashing the bus window to fly after the runaway pram.

The bus drew away from the stop. He pulled out his phone and texted Linda that he was on his way. This was the best part of the day, going home.

As usual, Symington had been too idle to put in the CCTV videos that recorded the bank overnight. He knew it was a sacking offence but he didn't understand the machines. The bank wasn't insured if the security devices weren't working, but Symington thought he was above the rules. Every night Kevin put new tapes into the machines before the bank closed and replaced them in the morning.

He could hear two women laughing as they climbed up to the top deck. He recognized one of their voices, and turned, slipping his mobile back into his coat pocket.

He hadn't seen Debbie Robinson since he had left school, almost fifteen years ago, but she had hardly changed. She still looked great and he felt shy, like he always had at school with her. She wore a black mini-skirt, biker boots and jacket. Her hair was jet black and punky, and she had the biggest blue eyes he had ever seen. She was chatting with her mate as they walked past him and took the seat in front. She didn't notice him. Just like at school, really.

Her mate's phone rang and she was soon talking about what pub to go to that night. Debs checked her hair in a compact mirror and caught Kevin looking at her in its reflection. She swung round. 'What the fuck d'ya— Hang on, I know you. You're Kevin . . . Kevin something or other. I remember you from school. You had one of those pogo-stick things, didn't you?'

'That was Kevin Logan. I'm Kevin Dodds.'

'Yeah, right.' She thought hard. 'Got it. The podgy one, basin haircut, always in the back row.'

Kevin was sort of pleased she knew who he was, but he was still a little nervous talking to her. 'So, what are you up to, Debs? Married with kids and a poodle?'

'Married with one kid. No poodle. You remember Dave, don't you? Captain of the football team? But you didn't play football at school, did you?'

Kevin shook his head. 'Er, no. But I knew him.'

Everyone at school had known Dave. He played almost every sport for the school. That made him hated by the boys as much as he was loved by the girls. Worse, he was good-looking, always had money and never got spots.

Debs's mate closed down her phone and listened to the conversation while she shoved salt and vinegar crisps into her mouth. Her crunching was nearly as loud as Debs's voice.

'Well, he's got his own carpet business in Leadenbridge now. Got lots of staff. Doing really well,' Debs went on.

Debs's friend wasn't impressed. She pulled a face. 'Yeah, Dave's doing really well and still just as popular. That's why he's never at home, eh, Debs?'

Debs shot her a look that told her to shut it. She shoved some more crisps into her mouth.

Kevin had played football at school but only with the other kids who never got picked for the team. It wasn't that he was bad at it. He just never looked right. He was a bit plump, as he was now, but it was more than that. All the other kids had the right Adidas shorts, and the right trainers. Kevin's mum always bought him cheap ones from the market. Even at ten, kids could pick out a loser.

Debs was still going on about Dave. 'Anyway, I married him, and we've just moved into the new Bovis estate. We got the show-home up there. It's gorgeous. Three bathrooms. I'm a hairdresser at Cuts To Go in town. What about you?'

'Remember Linda Perry? We've been married seven years now. No kids, and definitely no poodle. I'm the deputy manager at The Bank, the one on Middle Street.'

'Linda? Wasn't she the zitty one with greasy hair and Mr Magoo glasses?'

Debs's friend was giggling now. Debs nudged her. Kevin did what he normally did at times like this. He just smiled. He didn't want to make a scene. 'Dunno . . . Anyway, she doesn't have spots or glasses or greasy hair now.'

'I remember Linda.' Debs turned to her mate who was now munching a Mars bar. 'They were the school geeks, yeah? Ah. That's love for you.'

Her mate swallowed and let out a

high-pitched giggle.

Debs liked that and carried on taking the piss. 'Hey, Kev. You should do something about your hair. That side-parting just isn't on. Come and see me and I'll bring you into the nineteen nineties at least.' They stood up for their stop. The Mars bar wrapper and crisps packet were stuffed down the back of the seat. 'See ya, Kev. Listen, maybe don't bother with the cut. I'm sure the lovely Linda likes you just as you are, but what about some gel?'

Kevin heard more giggles as they disappeared down the stairs. No doubt Debs had made another joke about him. He should have said something back to her. But he hadn't been able to think of anything smart or witty. He was thirty this year, but it had been just like school. Some things never changed.

CHAPTER FIVE

Tesco was round the corner from Specsavers where Linda worked. She liked to meet him off the bus each night but as it was so cold and wet, Kevin had called her at lunchtime and said they would meet in the supermarket. They did their weekly shop on Friday nights.

Linda took the car to work as Specsavers had free staff parking round the back. Since Kevin finished work an hour earlier than she did, he took the bus to her so they could drive home together. He could have taken the bus all the way, but their ten-year-old Fiesta was on its last legs. Sometimes he had to get under the bonnet before it would start. Anyway, he liked to chat to Linda as they drove home together or went round the supermarket.

The next stop was his. As he got

up, he spotted Linda in the doorway of the dry cleaner's. She looked lovely in her black coat, with her shoulder-length dark brown hair blowing across her face. So what if they had been geeks at school? They weren't now. Or, at least, Linda wasn't. He loved her, and always had, even at school. But he had been twenty before he had plucked up the courage to ask her out.

Linda looked up and saw him. She waved and smiled, her cheeks pink with cold. Kevin felt so lucky to have her. He ran down the stairs, jumped off the bus and was in the doorway with her. They kissed and Linda opened her umbrella. The wind turned it inside out. Kevin helped her to put it right.

'Why didn't you wait in Tesco's? Look at you, you're all wet.'

They walked off arm in arm towards the supermarket.

'I wanted to make sure you didn't get too wet. I thought I'd come to the rescue with what's left of my umbrella,' Linda told him. Like Kevin, she always made every effort to spend a few extra minutes with her other half. Kevin felt a surge of love for her. Neither of them had ever been out with anyone else. So what if other people thought they were geeks? So long as they had each other, it didn't matter. Occasionally, Kevin would lie in bed in the middle of the night and worry about what life would be like if she wasn't there. What if she left him? Or got ill and died? 'Come on. Let's get the shopping done and go home,' he said.

As they walked up to Tesco, Kevin said, 'I just met Debs on the bus. From school, remember?'

Of course Linda remembered. Debs had been the really pretty punk that all the boys fancied and all the girls had wanted to look like. 'You fancied her, didn't you?'

'Nah, not really. Well, OK.

Everyone did. Not that she would have looked at me.'

'How is she? I never liked her.'

Kevin kept it brief. He didn't say Debs had been taking the piss out of his haircut. And his wife. 'She seemed OK, I suppose. Now, what shall we get for tea?'

CHAPTER SIX

The rain bounced off the windows of Kevin and Linda's house. It was a two-up, two-down Victorian terrace, nicely decorated in B&Q paints and nicely furnished by Ikea. They liked their home. It was warm and safe.

Kevin knew more about celebrity diets, liposuction and Oscar-night outfits than the average man should. Linda read gossip magazines. She always felt the need to share what she learned, so Kevin always knew what was hot and what was not. They finished off their microwave chicken dinner for two and cuddled up on the settee. Linda flicked through her latest magazine and Kevin picked up a holiday brochure. How could he tell her he still hadn't asked for the day off?

'What do you think of this, Kev?' Linda flapped the page under his nose.

'It's a woman in a long green dress.'

'It's Halle Berry. I'd love to look like her. Isn't her dress beautiful?'

'It's fine.'

'It's a bit better than that, Kev.'

'It's lovely, then.'

'You'll never make a fashion reporter.'

'And you'll never make a TV holiday presenter if you don't pick one out.' He bopped her on the head gently with the brochure. 'I'm wondering if we should look at your mum's caravan again. I know we really want Greece, but Southwold would be much cheaper. What do you think?'

Linda turned a few pages of blue skies and sea. 'Greece looks fantastic. Do you really fancy the caravan?'

'Not really. But there's the mortgage to pay, and that new car we keep talking about. Maybe we're pushing it this year.'

'OK. I'll ask her on Friday.' She put down the brochure. 'Hey, you know what, Kev? Maybe you should rob a bank instead of working in one.'

Kevin gave her a look that said, 'We never do bank-robbery jokes.'

'I know, I know! Only joking. But I was thinking about old George Rowland and all that cash he's got tucked away.'

'Don't you dare tell anyone I told you!' Kevin cut in. 'I'd lose my job!'

'But if your bank got robbed and all those safe-deposit boxes were opened, he wouldn't be able to tell anyone he'd had all that cash stolen, would he? Serve him right.'

She giggled.

'Just think if we had his money, Kev. We could pay off the mortgage, buy the car and a place in the sun, pay for my mum's treatment. I could even buy Halle Berry's green dress.'

'Yeah, yeah. Green dresses and tropical islands all round, eh?'

'Can't really see you in a green dress, Kev, but, yep, you get the idea.'

Kevin made a grab for her and started to tickle. She shrieked and tried to wriggle away. It turned into a hug.

'Hey, Kev, you get Friday off?'

'Not yet.'

Linda sat up and looked disappointed.

'I just didn't get the chance to ask him. I'll do it on Monday, first thing. Promise.'

Linda sighed. She'd been through this one before. 'Kev, please talk to him. It would be great to have a long weekend. It is our anniversary, darling. You've got to stand up for yourself a bit. You're practically running that bank. The least Symington can do is give you a day off. Besides, you're entitled to it. You haven't had any holiday yet.'

'I'll do it on Monday. I'm just not good at this sort of thing. He always reacts badly when people take single days off.'

'I know. But that's his problem, not yours. Please, Kevin.'

A silence followed and Kevin picked up the TV remote control. 'Come on,' he said. 'Give us a cuddle.'

Linda curled up beside him and rested her head on his shoulder as *Look East*, the BBC local news sparked up on the screen. A perky TV presenter announced that the actress Jessica Drake had arrived in Ipswich today. She was in town for a week to play a cameo role in Oscar

Wilde's *Lady Windermere's Fan*.

Kevin and Linda watched Jessica step out of her car as two men held umbrellas over her. The theatre was just down the road from the bank. He must have missed all the fuss this afternoon, he thought. She was very tall, very blonde, and very beautiful. She towered above the theatre director as they posed for photographers. Her necklace glittered in the camera's flash.

Kevin had never heard of Jessica Drake, but Linda had. 'Look! Isn't she stunning? And her necklace is amazing. You know all about the Augusta necklace, right?'

Clearly, he had missed a few pages of gossip. He shook his head, and waited to be filled in.

As Linda spoke her eyes never left the screen. 'The Augusta necklace is that string of pearls, with a sapphire and diamond clasp. See?' She pointed at the TV. 'You wear the clasp at the front. It's worth two million. I'd love to look like her.'

'You wanted to look like Halle Berry a minute ago. Make your mind up.' But Kevin could see that Jessica was indeed stunning. Shoulder-length hair, blue eyes, bee-stung lips.

'She's always so elegant. Imagine being able to wear a necklace like that. It was a present from her husband, Greg Drake, the film director.'

Kevin had never heard of Greg Drake either, but Linda was now in full flow. 'They only found out the necklace was worth a fortune when they were getting divorced.' She paused for breath, and the TV report took over the story.

Greg Drake had paid a thousand dollars for the necklace when he bought it from a jeweller in India. But during the messy divorce, it was valued at over two million pounds. Greg had wanted it back. He said it was an old family piece. But Jessica proved that he had given it to her when she turned thirty, and won.

Linda couldn't take her eyes off the TV. 'You'd feel like a princess in it.'

Kevin could see that the blue of the sapphire matched Jessica's eyes. Now, that's the kind of woman I should star with in my action movies, he thought. *Pulp Fiction* starring Jessica Drake and Kevin Dodds. He repeated it a couple of times in his head, but it didn't seem right. His name only worked with Linda's. *Pulp Fiction* starring Linda and Kevin Dodds. That was better.

Anyway, he'd rather be with Linda than Jessica. You could have a laugh with Linda, and Jessica didn't look like she'd let her hair down in a hurry. Besides, he wasn't cut out to be a movie star. He was the kind of man nobody noticed much. He didn't know why Linda wanted him. He was a grey man.

Kevin held Linda tighter as they lay on the settee and watched Jessica tell *Look East* how thrilled she was to be in Ipswich. 'Thought I'd finally put up those shelves for you tomorrow,' he said. 'Then I'll go into town and pick up a DVD.'

Linda's eyes were still on Jessica. 'I've got Legs, Bums and Tums at eleven. Then I've got to pick up Mum's dry-cleaning, and drop it round hers. See you about one?'

'You don't need to do that Bums and Tums thing.'

'I do if I'm going to look like Halle Berry for our holiday.'

'I like you looking like you do now.' He pulled her closer.

'You're such a smoothie. I love you.'

'Me too.'

'You can say it, you know, it doesn't bite.'

He smiled, but he didn't say it. He had no idea why he found it so hard to say those three words out loud. To him it sounded corny in the movies, and just as corny in real life. Anyway,

Linda knew he loved her. He was just no good at love talk. He was better at showing it through his actions. Like putting up shelves.

CHAPTER SEVEN

Saturday, 4 February, 10.17 a.m.

The rain had stopped overnight so at least Saturday shoppers didn't get wet as they went about the city centre. Kevin bit into a bacon sandwich, fresh from Bobby's Snacks on the market, and wiped a blob of tomato ketchup off his chin. Those shelves had looked dead easy to put up but it had taken him a couple of hours to get them level. Now, with Linda out of the way, he had a chance to buy her an anniversary present. He ate the rest of his sandwich and headed for the only jeweller he knew, Hearts on the high street. It was where he had bought Linda's wedding ring.

He had a quick look in the window but nothing grabbed him, apart from his reflection. Was the hair gel he had slipped into the shopping trolley last night making him look cool or not? Today his hair had a seriously spiky thing going on.

He went inside the shop, unsure of himself, and tried to avoid eye-contact with the two women behind the counter. He pretended to be interested in a display of men's watches with giant faces. Nothing for Linda there. He moved to a glass cabinet and couldn't believe his eyes. There, centre stage, was a beautiful pearl necklace. With a sapphire and diamond clasp.

'The Augusta,' a voice said, so close to his ear that he jumped. 'Wonderful, isn't it?' The sales woman had come round to the front of the counter.

'It's lovely.' Kevin pointed at it.

37

'Are they real?'

'The pearls are cultured ones, which makes them cheaper. The jewels are glass, but good quality, as you can see. The actress Jessica Drake got her mitts on the real thing. Did you know she's in Ipswich for a play?'

'I saw her on the news last night.'

'Well, after everyone saw her wearing it for the first time, these necklaces became all the rage. It was a few years ago now, but the design is timeless.'

It was stunning. Not that Kevin was a jewel expert, but he knew Linda would love it. He squinted at the tiny price tag. Five hundred and seventy pounds. He'd only saved two hundred and fifty. His hand shook a little as he reached for his wallet. He knew it was a dumb thing to do, but he'd put the rest on his card. It was just too good to miss. He imagined Linda beaming as she opened it.

Common sense flew out of the

window. 'I'll take it,' he whispered.

Kevin's next stop was Marco's. 'Hi, Mark. I just want to confirm you've still got my table for next Saturday at—'

Mark smiled and held up his hand. He didn't need to double-check his book. He had made the booking for Kevin last week when he had popped in, just as he had last year and all the years before that. Lovely couple. 'Anniversary time again, is it, Mr Dodds?'

'Yes.'

'You have a new hairstyle, I see.' Kevin waited to hear what Mark thought of it.

'We'll look forward to seeing you both on Saturday, Mr Dodds.'

'Me too.' Kevin turned to the door, then stopped. 'Maybe you could help me do something a little special this time, Mark . . .'

Almost home. Just one last stop— Blockbuster—and then he was done for the day. Like some people can lose track of time reading, gardening or playing football, Kevin could spend all day in Blockbuster. Films were his passion. He liked to scan the shelves for hidden treasure. Something he might not have seen before, maybe an old black-and-white, an Italian thriller, or a cops-and-robbers B movie.

Linda always went to bingo on a Saturday night to keep her mum company, and Kevin stayed in to watch DVDs. Apart from next week, of course, when Linda was going to bingo on Friday.

Kevin looked along the shelves for old favourites, like they were long-lost friends. His finger hovered over *Blackhawk Down*. He must have seen it twenty times, but it was worth watching another twenty. He had learned quite a lot about life from watching films. The way he dealt with Symington came from an old black-and-white prison film. The prisoner had just smiled and taken whatever the guard threw at him so that the older men got beaten less often.

He limited himself to one DVD a week, and choosing just one was part of the fun. You had to think about what mood you were in, what would satisfy you most on that particular night. Narrowing the choice gave the game an edge. Usually he plumped for an action film and today was no exception. His finger traced along the shelves. Maybe *Pulp Fiction*. Maybe *The Bourne Identity*. Or maybe *Training Day*. Or what about *Butch Cassidy and the Sundance Kid*? Just the movie for when you were in the mood for a western, except he wasn't. No, let's save that. Hang on. Here was an old favourite. *The Score*, a bank-robbery film starring Robert de Niro.

*　　　*　　　*

As he unlocked the front door, Linda

came out of the kitchen. Her hair was freshly washed after her gym class and she looked good in jeans and a black polo-neck.

'What's with the hair?'

'Er, I gelled it.'

'I can see that.'

'Like it?'

'Yeah, it's . . . well . . . it's fine.' They burst out laughing. 'Nah.' They shook their heads and laughed even more.

Kevin leaped up the stairs. 'I'll go and wash it.'

He laughed all the way to the bedroom, then pulled out a long black box from under his jacket. Before he hid it behind the wardrobe, he couldn't resist taking a peep.

The Augusta pearls gleamed up at him against the blue velvet lining. He snapped the box shut in case he gave it to her there and then. He buried the thought of next month's credit-card bill.

'Be down in a minute!' he called.

CHAPTER EIGHT

Monday, 6 February, 10.24 a.m.

Kevin gazed out of the bank's window at tall grey buildings with thick grey clouds pressing down on them. Not much going on out there. He looked back to the computer screen—also grey—and wondered how he would get through the next six hours.

Symington had given him the cleaning bill for his suit and stuck him on the counter as Margaret was sick, but he'd been there for an hour and so far only two customers had come in. It wasn't his job to cover now that he'd been promoted. Gary and Alice were supposed to do that, but Symington put Kevin back at the counter whenever he could. It was one of his ways of keeping Kevin in his place. As always, Kevin smiled and got on with the job.

Gary and Alice were behind him now, sitting at the main desk checking paperwork. They occasionally looked up from their print-outs to share a joke. Kevin tapped his pencil on the counter as if to magic a queue of people into the bank, but still no one came.

Kevin could see Symington by the fax machine. A piece of paper was jammed in it—his boss was hopping from one foot to the other, opening and closing the lid.

Now was Kevin's chance. He leaped up and dashed over. 'Something jammed, Mr Symington? Need a hand?'

'Stupid machine isn't working. Every time I press start, three red lights flash on but nothing happens.'

'Let's have a look.' Kevin lifted the lid and wiggled the piece of paper that was trapped inside. It came out easily. He reset the start button, inserted the fax and hit send. The machine started to dial.

'Glad to see you've got a talent for something.'

It was now or never. He'd promised Linda. 'Mr Symington, could I ask you something if you have a moment?'

'You've got until this fax goes through or until we have a customer.'

'I wondered if I could take this Friday off.' Symington's eyebrows rose an inch. 'You see, it's my wedding anniversary on Saturday and—'

Symington's hand went to his moustache and started to twirl. He enjoyed having Kevin on a hook. 'A bit late to ask for a day off, isn't it? I always demand five working days' notice if this bank is to function properly. You should have asked me before the weekend.'

'I know, but it's still four days' notice and it's been so quiet lately.'

'Ah, that's the nature of banking, Kevin. One moment it's quiet, and the next it's all hands on deck. You just never know what's going to happen.' He waved his arm across the silent room.

'Well, Margaret said she'd be back on Friday. I've checked with Gary and Alice and they're happy to cover for me, but I really don't think it will be that busy.'

As soon as he said it, he knew he'd made a mistake. 'You don't think it'll be busy. And who are you? The Mystic Meg of banking? You're not paid to *think*, Kevin. You're paid to *do*. I'll do the thinking around here, and *I* think it may be busy. Sorry, Kevin, but rules are rules. Give me five days' notice in future, and I'll see what I can do.'

'But—'

'No buts, Kevin. I'm sorry, we'll need you here on Friday.'

Kevin wanted to say more, but he couldn't think of anything. He couldn't ask for next Monday off as Linda was on a training day. Fed up, he plodded back to his stool and sat down. A wave of misery washed through him. Why couldn't he stand up to Symington for once in his life?

The next two and a half hours dragged. Three people came in. Two to make deposits and an old lady who thought she was in the Halifax next door. He filled in the time by double-checking the safe-deposit records on the computer. He stopped for a sandwich. Then there were another two and a half hours of boredom to get through. Dull. Dull. Dull.

CHAPTER NINE

Monday, 6 February, 4.30 p.m.

Kevin, who had been clock-watching all day, knew the exact time when the two women burst into the bank. 'You were supposed to have fixed this yesterday!' the taller one yelled. 'I sometimes wonder what I'm paying you for! Never mind. As usual, I'll do it myself.'

Kevin recognized her from the TV straight away. She was tall, slim, with glossy blonde hair and very high cheekbones. As soon as she saw him watching her, her frown was replaced with a smile. She took a deep breath, and came slowly up to the counter, as if she was on a catwalk. She was wearing a black fur coat with high heels, and her hips swayed as she moved. Her assistant remained five paces behind.

Jessica stopped at Kevin's window and peeled off her black leather gloves. 'Hello.' Her voice was rich and low. 'My name is Jessica Drake.'

Kevin's eyes were glued to her collarbone. She was wearing the Augusta necklace. 'Good afternoon, madam.' He sounded a bit stiff, like Symington.

'Darling, you probably know that I'm performing at the Theatre Royal, just down the road from you. Well, I can't leave my necklace in the wings while I'm on stage, or some wicked little chorus girl will steal it. I thought I'd better deposit it in your bank for the week. My assistant will pick it up on Monday morning. Would that be possible, darling?'

As she talked, Kevin stared at the necklace. He was trying to fix all of the details in his head so he could remember them for Linda later. Jessica Drake was just as beautiful in real life as she was on TV. She had pale, clear skin and bright blue eyes with the longest eyelashes he'd ever seen. But there was something odd about her face. It was so smooth, it didn't seem to move as she spoke. It was as if someone was pulling the skin at the back of her head. And when you looked closely, the lashes at the outer corners of her eyes went a bit too far beyond each eye. And her lips seemed too big and a bit sore . . .

'Darling, are you listening? I want to deposit my Augusta. I assume your bank offers a safe-deposit service?'

'Of course, madam. If you'd like to walk over to the door on your right, I'll buzz you straight through. There's just a little paperwork.'

'OK, but hurry up, darling, I'm in rather a rush.'

Jessica headed towards the door. Kevin felt a stab of nerves as he went to meet her. He was doing business with a Hollywood movie star. Well, sort of. Linda had told him Jessica hadn't been in a film since her divorce, but that didn't matter. His wife would still be dead impressed.

By the look of it, so were his workmates. They had stopped what they were doing and their mouths hung open.

Jessica was every inch the movie star, but the necklace was what drew your eye. The two strands of pearls glowed, and the sapphire and diamonds twinkled. Kevin's present for Linda looked just like the real thing!

He pressed the security switch and the door unlocked.

'My driver is waiting outside,' snapped Jessica. 'I can't be long. Must I really sign some silly form? After all, you do know who I am?'

Kevin held open the door for her as she glided in with her assistant. 'Yes, of course I do. I saw you on TV last Friday. But I'm afraid we can't take a deposit without filling in a form. Sorry.'

'You saw me on TV, did you? You'd think the media would have had enough of me by now, but they always seem to want more. Oh, well.' She stroked her fur coat. 'I guess that's just the downside of being famous.'

'Madam, please.' He took her into his office where he kept the forms. 'Do sit down. Can I take your coat?'

This was turning into an exciting day. Kevin couldn't wait to tell Linda about it. He wondered if he could ask Jessica for an autograph. Maybe it wasn't the right thing to do. But what was the harm? He'd ask her when the necklace was safely in the basement.

'Forget my coat. Just get on with it!' She sat down and slowly crossed one long leg over the other. The other woman stood beside her. 'Quickly! Give me the forms.' Jessica pointed to her assistant. Clearly, you didn't pass anything to royalty in person.

Kevin handed them to the assistant with his pen, and the two women signed their names.

'Don't just stand there, sweetheart. Fetch me the key.' Her voice wasn't quite so rich and low now that she had only him to watch her. It was more of a screech.

Kevin unlocked the safe fixed to the wall behind him.

In it, there was a row of small hooks with numbers underneath. Some had a key hanging from them, but many didn't as the client kept their key at home. At the top of the safe, there was a small shelf with just one key. This was the guard key for all the boxes.

Each deposit box had two locks, which had to be unlocked before the box would open. The guard key was kept in the safe, and used by Kevin to open the first lock. Then Kevin would leave the guard key in the lock and the client used their own key to open the second. Kevin had to leave the guard key in the lock because the client's key would only work if the guard was in place. It was extra security so that the two locks couldn't be picked.

The safe in Kevin's office also had two locks to open and close it. Symington held the guard key and Kevin had the second. Each morning Symington would open his lock, then Kevin opened his. At the end of the day, they both locked the safe for the night.

'Come on, then.' Jessica snatched the little key out of his hand. 'Show me my box.'

'It's downstairs, if you'd like to follow me. Oh, I should have introduced myself. I'm Kevin Dodds, deputy manager.'

Jessica looked put out. 'Deputy manager? I thought you were the manager. I can't hand over my necklace to any Tom, Dick or Harry. I insist on dealing with the manager.'

'I look after deposits, madam, and

you don't need to hand your necklace to me. You can lock it into the safe yourself and keep the key, so that you can be sure it's all in order.'

'I know that.' She looked Kevin up and down. 'I've had more safe-deposit boxes than you've had hot dinners, but I will not be taken care of by a deputy. It's like going to the theatre and getting the understudy, you silly little man.'

She slapped the top of his desk. 'Fetch me the manager. Now!'

Kevin smiled and went to look for Symington in his office.

Symington dropped his newspaper when Kevin told him who wanted to see him and scuttled out to meet the star.

'Oh, there you are, darling. I told him I could only deal with the manager.' Jessica looked out of Kevin's office window to check that the other staff were watching. There was nothing she liked more than making a scene. 'Now, let's go and put away my Augusta. Perhaps you'd be kind enough to take it off me.'

Symington's eyes were very wide. He could only nod. Then, as if she were on stage, Jessica pulled off her coat and flung it at Kevin. 'Make yourself useful.'

She turned the clasp to the back of her neck and lifted her hair for Symington to undo the catch. Even from where he was standing, Kevin could hear his boss breathing heavily. Kevin was seriously pissed off. Deposits were his job. He had really wanted to undo the clasp of a two-million-pound necklace.

Symington handed the necklace to Jessica, who placed it in a black box that her assistant pulled out from her bag. 'Madam, if you'd like to follow me, I'll show you to your deposit box downstairs. Dodds, look after Ms Drake's coat.'

Jessica took the box from her assistant and headed for the stairs with the bank manager. Kevin heard

Symington's voice as they went down to the basement. 'I do apologize for my deputy. He's not very bright, and tends to get a bit star-struck.'

'Darling, he was no problem. I'm used to it. It's just nice to have the manager in charge of such an important deposit. Besides, that deputy of yours has his hands full now. He looks like a yeti all covered with fur.'

He heard them chuckle as they trotted down the stairs. Jessica's assistant took the coat from him and Kevin made his way back to the counter. He felt pleased that the great Jessica Drake hadn't been in any films for a long time. He was glad she had to travel up and down the country just to get a small part in a small town. She was a bitch.

CHAPTER TEN

It hadn't been a great start to the week for Kevin. By the end of the day, all he wanted was to get home and spend a relaxing evening with Linda. In the car he put on their favourite Billy Joel tape, the one with their song on it, hoping she wouldn't ask him if he had managed to get Friday off. He knew she'd ask, but he wanted a few minutes' peace before the storm.

When they were sitting on the sofa drinking tea and watching *EastEnders*, she still hadn't asked. Kevin realized he was going to have to tell her, and ruin the evening. He waited until the end of the programme.

'I'm sorry, Linda. I asked Symington for the day off, but he said no.'

Linda's face flushed. He could see

she was trying to control her anger. 'But he can't do that. He's no right. You're entitled to a day off. It's just not fair.'

'He said we're just too busy.'

'Busy? When's that place ever busy?'

'I know, but I gave four days' notice and the rules say I have to give five.'

He could see that her annoyance had transferred from Symington to him.

'I told you you should have done it last week. I was really looking forward to this weekend. It's our anniversary.'

'I know. I'm so sorry. I was waiting for the right time to ask him.' He put a hand on her knee. 'I'm really sorry. At least we've still got the weekend.'

Linda could see he was upset too and knew it was pointless to go on at him. Kevin was almost too gentle, too nice. She'd tried to encourage him to stand up for himself a bit more, push himself forward a bit, but he never seemed able to do it. It meant people walked all over him. She needed to help him build his self-confidence. She knew he had it in him to be more forceful. Maybe one day the penny would finally drop.

'Something else happened today, though.' Kevin changed the subject. 'Guess who came into the bank.' He had saved the good news to tell her after the bad.

'Who?'

'Jessica Drake.'

'No! You're kidding me! Was she wearing it?'

'Yep—and a big fur coat.'

'What's it like? What's *she* like? What else was she wearing?' Now she was caught up in a real-life gossip mag. 'I can't believe you've met Jessica Drake! Wait till I tell the girls at work. How big was the sapphire?'

Kevin made a rock-sized circle

with his thumb and index finger. 'She had the world's most stunning necklace, but she wasn't the world's most stunning woman. My wife is.'

Linda grinned and shuffled up next to him on the sofa. 'Of course,' she said, pleased. 'Come here.'

As they kissed, he realized it was true. Linda was more beautiful than Jessica. She was natural, and lovely, and kind. Far better than that fake, second-rate actress. He hugged her closer.

And then it happened. Today became the day that Kevin Dodds got angry. Really angry. He didn't know if it was because Symington wouldn't give him the day off, or because Jessica Drake had thrown her coat at him, or even because he'd seen his wife's disappointment in him. But while he was sitting on the sofa and Linda was waffling on about the Augusta, the dam burst. He felt pure anger twist and spread through his body until he was filled with rage.

He clenched his fists, his breathing came fast and the blood rushed to his head. He didn't have to live like this. He didn't have to take it all lying down. He could fight back. It was time to stop being the grey man.

Slowly a plan began to hatch.

Linda glanced at him. 'What are you grinning at?'

'Just thinking about Saturday night, that's all. I'm going to make it the most wonderful night you've ever had. I'll make up for not getting Friday off, I promise.'

And for the first time Kevin's life got interesting.

CHAPTER ELEVEN

Tuesday, 7 February, 11.28 a.m.

For Gary and Alice, today was like any other day at the bank. There was the usual lack of customers and

Symington shouting at them every now and again. But for Kevin today wasn't an ordinary day. He was in his office, with his paperwork in front of him, and his mug of coffee in his hand, but today was the day that would change his life for ever.

He paused for a moment, his finger hovering over the mouse. Google's search engine was on screen and he had already typed in 'home-made explosives'. If he clicked, Kevin knew there would be no turning back. He was terrified, but he'd had enough of people walking all over him. He'd had enough of smiling. It was now or never. He was going to do something that Robert de Niro, and Clint Eastwood had done loads of times. He was going to rob a bank. He took a long, deep breath, and then the grey man struck back. He clicked the mouse.

The first page of home-made explosives was on the screen but before Kevin had a chance to start reading, Symington burst into his office. 'Dodds! Why aren't you out there making sure those two are doing their work?'

Kevin stood behind his desk hoping that Symington wouldn't walk round it and see what was on the screen. He peered out through his door and saw Alice at the counter doing paperwork. Gary was making a phone call.

'Well, er . . . Alice can handle the counter. And Gary's making business calls. It's not busy so I thought I'd start this month's report early.'

Symington wasn't too sure how to react to that one. 'Good.' He left Kevin's office and stormed back to his own. Kevin closed the door and got back to his PC.

He checked out a number of websites that showed him how to make explosives before it dawned on him. Why was he looking at all this stuff? He didn't know the first thing about blowing up safe-deposit boxes. He'd probably blow himself up instead. As Clint had said to him one Saturday night, 'A man's got to know his limitations.'

Kevin sat back in his chair and thought about his. He didn't have a clue about what he was doing. He had no experience in such matters. Except that he'd watched a hundred and one bank-robbery movies, the good ones at least twice. He wasn't fit, so the chance of him swinging above motion detectors by his finger-nails, wasn't good. And he wasn't a genius, so he was unlikely to come up with a plan no one else had ever thought of. No, his plan would depend on two things. First, it should need no brains and no fitness, and second, it used the one advantage he did have. He was already in the bank and knew how the systems worked.

He closed down Google and rested his elbows on the desk, dropping his head into his hands. He knew the exact safe-deposit box he was going to break into, but how to do it without anyone knowing he had? That was the problem. After all, it wasn't as if he was going to run away with Linda to a tropical island. If a theft was obvious, the police would soon have him as a suspect. After all, Kevin had keys to the bank and dealt with the deposit boxes every day. He didn't know how he would stand up to their questions. Would he confess out of fear? Would guilt be written all over his face? He never had been a good liar. No, this had to be a crime that no one ever knew had been committed. So, no alarms, no noisy explosives, no bits of broken deposit-box strewn across the floor. It had to be a clean, silent crime that no one ever knew about.

Kevin had a sip of coffee to wake himself up. Even if he could get to the safe-deposit box with the guard key, he would still need the client key to open it. How was he going to get his hands on it?

Symington was outside his door again, moaning at Gary, who had offered to cover for Kevin on Friday. 'This is a place of work, not a charity.'

Kevin felt the anger twist in his belly. He was going to put his plan into action this Friday evening. He was looking forward to coming into work on Monday morning. Symington and everyone else would be none the wiser as to what had taken place. But he'd go back to his plan later. Now he had to start on that report. After all, he'd said he would.

CHAPTER TWELVE

After work, Kevin met Linda at Specsavers as usual, and they drove home together. Instead of their usual banter, they were silent. Linda was worried about Kevin. He seemed distant, as if he was in another world. Maybe he was tired.

The rest of the evening should have felt normal but it didn't. Kevin sat and watched TV with Linda as usual and cuddled her as usual. But Linda could feel that something wasn't right. Kevin's thoughts were elsewhere. He replied to anything she asked him with a one-word answer. Otherwise he didn't speak at all.

Something was wrong. Linda could feel it. Maybe it was work . . . but maybe it was her. Had she done something to upset him? She kept her head on his chest so she didn't have to look him in the eye as the ten o'clock news started. 'You OK, Kev? You've been really quiet all night.'

He stroked her hair. He had been thinking about the plan that was now forming in his head. 'Course I am.' He kissed her. 'I'm fine. Just worried about some extra work I've got to do.'

'Symington cocked up again?'

'Yeah, sort of.'

Linda was relieved it wasn't something she had done. 'Come on.' She pulled herself to her feet. 'Bed.'

'I think I'd better make a start on it now. I have to get some stuff done by Friday. You go on. I'll be up in a bit.'

Linda went to bed but lay on her back looking up at the ceiling. Things still didn't feel right. Kevin didn't worry about work. She rolled over, switched off the lamp and tried to go to sleep.

*　　　*　　　*

Kevin was back online with his mate Google. He knew what the client lock looked like, but didn't have a clue what sort it was, or how it worked. Hopefully Google would show him. He had worked out a sort of plan, but a million things were buzzing around in his mind and they had to be put into order. Kevin wasn't fazed by that. OK, so he was used to dealing with bank stuff, not robbery, but he was sure the basic idea had to be similar. A bit like when he had to decide if a customer could have a loan. If he wasn't sure, he got more information. He clicked enter.

Google came up with hundreds of different locks. It took some time but Kevin finally found what he was looking for.

Kevin sat back in his chair, pleased with himself. It was like being in a film. If it was a western, he would have been wearing a poncho and sucking at a big fat cigar. Just like Clint.

CHAPTER THIRTEEN

Now Kevin knew how the client's lock worked, he had to find out how to pick it open. He clicked through more websites and found out that he didn't need to know. A company in Holland could send him a machine that would do the job for him. He punched in his credit-card details and pressed 'Purchase Now'. As the order went through, he felt a wave of fear. Not only had he left a record on his own PC about lock-picking, and looked up explosives on his work PC, he had given his credit-card number and taken action. There would be a record of it. If anything went wrong with his plan and the robbery was discovered, he would end up in jail. Still, if it didn't worry de Niro in *The Score*, then it shouldn't worry him. He would just have to make sure that he wasn't caught.

Time for tea and a KitKat. As he went to the kitchen drawer and pulled out the biscuit tin, he thought of the safe-deposit box's guard key. During the day, he had easy access to it since it was in his office safe. But even if Kevin could pick the client lock with his Dutch kit, he wouldn't be able to do it in office hours. Symington had the CCTV security screens in his office and would see him 'attacking' the client lock. He felt pleased with himself. He had just used a real lock-picker's expression. He was becoming a pro.

Even if Symington was doing his crossword and not looking up at the time, Kevin would still be on film. If there was an incident in the bank that day, if a customer slipped on a wet floor and hurt himself, the tape would have to be sent to Head Office in case the customer sued the bank. Kevin had to make sure he wasn't on any CCTV tape before he attacked the lock. He would have to do it at night when there was no risk of a customer problem. He wouldn't put the tapes in the recorders on Friday night.

He made the tea, and as he took the first bite of his KitKat, Linda appeared in her dressing-gown. 'You sure you're OK, Kev? I'm sorry for getting angry last night. It's Symington, not you. Is it really just work? I haven't done anything wrong, have I? I mean, you never stay up and—'

'I'm sorry. I'm not really working.'

Tears started to fall down her cheeks. Kevin put down his mug and rushed over to her. 'It's OK. It's nothing bad. You remember last night when I promised you the best Saturday night ever?'

She nodded.

'Well, it's a secret, and it's going to take a little work to set up. That's all. You go to bed and keep out of my way for a bit, so I can get on.' He held her close and stroked her hair until she'd calmed down. 'It's OK. I'll be up in a minute.'

'I was really worried. Look at me, crying, but . . .'

Kevin walked with her to the stairs. 'It's OK. Anyway, you look beautiful when you cry. Take my tea—I'll be up soon.'

Kevin could hear Linda up in the bedroom as he got back online. Maybe all those Saturday nights spent watching movies and eating toffee-covered popcorn were going to pay off after all.

CHAPTER FOURTEEN

Wednesday, 8 February, 06.48 a.m.

Kevin was up and dressed much earlier than usual as he knew he had a lot to do before he went to work. He had barely slept. His mind had been too active. He had his regular tea and toast for breakfast, and was pouring the milk over Linda's sugar-free muesli when she came into the kitchen.

She kissed him. 'You're up early,' she said.

'Yeah, got to go. I've got stuff to do before Saturday night.'

'What stuff?'

He picked up his briefcase. 'You'll see.'

They normally went to work separately and today was no exception. Kevin took the number-eleven bus, but didn't get off at his usual stop. Today he was going to get off seven stops later, at B&Q. He put his briefcase on the seat beside him and opened it. He took out one of Linda's compact mirrors.

The compact was square, with two mirrors. He slid them out of the compact, then pulled out the clasp that held the sides together when it was closed. Now the compact was empty, and there was a hole where the clasp had been. He stuffed everything back into his briefcase. He'd need the compact, but he would chuck away the other bits later.

Last night, he had lain in bed putting his thoughts in order. He was working on de Niro's bank-robbing idea in *The Score*. The simpler the plan, the more likely it was to work. Kevin had come up with a simple five-step plan:

1. He wouldn't put any videos into the CCTV recorder on Friday before the bank closed for the weekend.
2. He would wait for Linda to leave for bingo on Friday, then head back to the bank. He would open the door and switch off the alarm by entering his pin number on the pad, just as he did in the morning when he got in first.
3. He would open the safe in his

office and take the guard key for the deposit box.

4. He would go down to the basement and open the guard lock on the deposit box and leave the key in place while he picked the client lock and took the contents of the black box.

5. He'd lock everything up again, then go home so that he was there before Linda got back from bingo at around ten thirty.

There were still two problems to be solved. First, he had to open the office safe without Symington's key. That was where the compact and B&Q came in. Second, he had to pick the client lock, and that was where the Dutch kit would come in. The website had told Kevin it would be with him in two days.

Out of the window, Kevin could see the morning traffic battling into work. It felt good not to be a commuter today—or, at least, not for a while. Right now he was a real bank robber. He felt a rush of excitement. Sitting around him, office workers were reading their papers and listening to their ipods, but he wasn't. He was on his way to buy stuff to make a key just like Symington's.

He reached the stop near B&Q and ran across the car park. Even at that time of the morning it was busy with builders loading up for the day. A quick whiz round the aisles and he'd be done.

Kevin was more than fifteen minutes late for work. He had had to fill the compact with the modelling clay he'd just bought before he got the bus. Then the traffic was bad on the way into the city. Out of breath, he raced into the bank. He had run all the way from the bus stop. His briefcase was full of the stuff he had bought from B&Q and he hid it all in his desk drawers. As he was putting away the clay-filled compact,

Symington burst in. 'This is a place of work, Dodds! You can't just come and go as you please.'

Kevin was standing behind his desk. The drawer was open, crammed with B&Q bags. 'I'm sorry, Mr Symington. The traffic was—'

Symington turned and walked out. 'You have work to do. Get on with it.'

Kevin closed the drawer and left his office to help Gary prepare the counter for the public.

Gary nodded towards Symington's office. 'I see he's in a good mood again.'

'Yeah, nothing changes.' Kevin tried to sound casual, because for him of course, everything had changed.

Symington was sitting at his desk with the *Daily Telegraph* spread out before him. He didn't look up as Kevin walked behind him to get to the cupboard with the video recorders. He replaced the three tapes and took a deep breath. Then he turned to make his first attempt at getting his hands on his boss's safe key. His mouth was dry.

'If you're busy, Mr Symington, I can open the safe for you.'

Symington closed the paper to reveal a bunch of keys beneath it. The safe key was on the key-ring, just inches away from him. Kevin needed it for just a few seconds.

'What did you say?'

'I'll open the safe for you. I'm going back to my office now.'

Symington waved him away with one hand and the other slipped the keys into his desk drawer. 'I'll be along in a minute. You've got your own work to do.'

Kevin worked through the lunch-hour and Gary brought him a sandwich. All morning he'd been waiting for a chance to get to Symington's key. Symington had gone for lunch but must have taken his keys with him. Kevin had checked the man's office after he had left.

Now it was early afternoon. He started to panic. What if he never got them? If he did, what if he was caught making the copy? He was starting to have second thoughts about the whole idea. Planning the job was one thing, but doing it was something else.

Symington came back from lunch and headed for his office. Ten minutes later, Kevin saw him come out and go downstairs to the toilets. Now was his chance. He grabbed the compact from his drawer and walked quickly, but not too quickly, into Symington's office.

The keys were where he'd thought they would be. He took them out of the drawer and, with trembling hands, opened the compact. He pressed the safe key into the clay, exactly in the centre. He squeezed the two halves of the compact together, slowly but firmly, just as the website had said.

'Gary! Your tie is loose.' Symington's voice was getting louder. He was heading for his office. Kevin's hands shook harder. The compact and the keys clattered on to the carpet. Shit. *Shit*. SHIT.

'Yes, a lovely day, Mrs Wright.' The office door burst open. 'What are you doing in here?'

Kevin stood by the desk and kicked the compact and keys under it. 'I—I—well, I just wanted to say I was sorry for being late this morning. It won't happen again.'

'Well, make sure of it. Now leave me to get on with my work. There's a lot to do.'

Kevin went to the door.

'Dodds, get me a coffee, would you?'

CHAPTER FIFTEEN

Kevin went to make the coffee. He could feel the blood pumping in his neck. His chest felt tight. It was hard to breathe. Cold sweat had broken out all over his body.

He could hardly control his shaking hands as he held the kettle under the tap. He didn't know what to do. He was terrified. He paced up and down the small kitchen while he waited for the water to boil. Any minute now Symington would be screaming his name when he found what lay under his desk. 'Shit, shit, *shit.*'

Alice came in to hang up her coat after lunch. 'You OK, Kev?' The kettle clicked off. 'You don't look too good. He giving you a hard time again?'

Kevin made Symington's coffee. 'I'm just a bit tired. Got a lot on my mind.'

Alice nodded as she left him. 'Know the feeling.'

He had to stop panicking, and work out how to get the compact back before Symington spotted it.

Symington was on the far side of his office when Kevin went in with the coffee. He was delving into his filing cabinet. Kevin went towards him. 'Here you are, Mr Symington. I hope it's strong enough for you—whoa!' He tripped over the bin again.

The coffee splashed down the back of the bank manager's jacket. 'You damned fool! What's wrong with you?' Symington tore it off as Kevin dropped to his knees to pick up the mug, which had rolled across the floor. 'I'm so sorry—I didn't see the bin again. So sorry Mr Symington. Are you OK? I'll pay for the cleaning.'

'You should open an account at the dry-cleaners.'

Kevin reached over to the box of tissues on Symington's desk and pulled out a wad. 'Here, let me help you.'

Symington snatched it from him, and started to dab at his jacket. Kevin grabbed another handful of tissues and began to mop the carpet, the desktop and drawers. 'I don't know what came over me. I'm so sorry. I'll clear it all up for you.'

'Get out of my sight. Send Alice in. She'll make a better job of it.'

'Yes, sir.' Kevin stuffed the tissues into his pocket and left the room.

Gary and Alice had heard the whole thing. Alice smiled at Kevin as he mouthed, 'Sorry.' She went into Symington's office. Gary swivelled on his stool at the counter and gave Kevin a thumbs-up. Kevin shrugged and went back into his office.

He closed the door and leaned against it. Then he allowed himself a slight smile. It had worked. He took the tissues out of his pocket, then put his hand back in and pulled out the compact. Separating the bunch of keys from the compact and putting them back into the desk drawer had been a nightmare. Maybe it was because his hands were trembling so much. He opened it and saw a perfect print of the key. His smile became broader. This was it. He'd copied the safe key. He was going to rob the bank!

*   *   *

That evening was much like the last one. Linda tried to talk to him, but Kevin was barely speaking. He had told her he had to stay up late again as he had more to do on the computer.

'Don't be too long,' she said, as she went up to bed.

When she'd gone, Kevin turned on the oven and placed the closed compact on the top shelf. It would take forty minutes for the clay to harden. Meanwhile he opened the tin of wood-filler he had also bought at B&Q and turned on the hob. He had a bit of cooking to do. He heated the filler until it became a brown liquid.

When the clay had hardened, he poured it into the print of the key. His website had told him it would harden overnight. He slipped it into his briefcase and washed up.

In bed, he couldn't sleep. He felt scared, excited too.

Linda's eyes were closed, but she was awake. She wasn't excited. She was just scared.

CHAPTER SIXTEEN

Thursday, 9 February, 12.27 p.m.

Kevin was at his desk. His door was closed and he was almost whispering into his mobile. 'But you said it would be here today.'

The Dutch woman at the end of the line was calm. She was used to anxious customers. 'But today isn't over yet, sir. I'll keep checking for your delivery time. If you give me your mobile number, I'll text you with the details.' Kevin gave it to her, then closed his phone.

It hadn't been a good morning. He took a deep breath and stood up, ready to go to lunch. Keep calm, Kev. He picked up his briefcase and made for the door. You've still got stuff to do.

With a prawn sandwich in one hand and the brown, now hardened, copy of the safe key in the other, he handed it to Greg at the heel bar.

'Thanks for the overdraft, Mr Dodds. It's been pretty quiet for this time of year. I'm hoping things will pick up, come spring.'

'No problem, Greg. It'll get busy. I'm sure of it.'

Greg looked at the strange brown

shape, then put it into the clamp of the cutting machine. 'It's from an old safe key, isn't it?'

Kevin munched his sandwich, more out of fear than hunger. 'It's my mother-in-law's. She lost the key but for some reason she had this copy stashed away. Why she didn't just get a proper spare cut in the first place, I don't know.' Kevin was flapping. He took another bite of sandwich to keep himself quiet and checked his mobile for texts. He knew he hadn't got one because the phone would have bleeped, but he couldn't stop himself.

Greg finished cutting the key and handed it to him with the copy. 'I thought for a minute you might be planning to rob your own bank!'

'How did you guess? It was meant to be a secret. How much?'

'On the house, Mr Dodds. And thanks again.'

CHAPTER SEVENTEEN

During the rest of the afternoon Kevin found it impossible to work. He checked his watch. 4.06 p.m. Holland was an hour ahead and he still hadn't had a text. He called again and the same woman answered. 'Look, I just need to know if it's here. Can I collect it yet?'

'As I've already explained, sir, I'm trying to find out where it is in the delivery chain. As soon as I know, I will text you.'

*   *   *

Kevin and Linda didn't have much to say to each other all evening. They still lay together on the settee, but Linda was only half watching the TV, and Kevin kept checking his mobile for texts.

Then it happened! Four bleeps

blasted out from Kevin's mobile. He nearly kicked Linda off the settee as he got up. The Dutch kit was on its way and could be picked up from the courier's depot any time after eleven tomorrow morning. He would fetch it during the lunch hour.

'Who's the text from, Kev?' Linda was watching him as he put the phone on the mantelpiece and headed for the kitchen.

'Er, just someone about Saturday night. You'll have to wait, remember? Want some tea?' He left the room.

Linda sat on the settee and stared at his mobile. She had never read any of his texts or emails before, but now she walked over and picked up the phone. Nothing. He had deleted it.

The rest of the evening carried on as before until they both went up to bed and fell asleep. Well, Kevin pretended he was asleep. In fact, he was going over his plan. Tonight he felt no excitement, just pure fear. He thought about all the heroes he had seen on-screen and tried to work out if they had been scared. He felt better when he remembered that many of them had. He cuddled into Linda and waited for the hours to pass.

Linda felt him behind her but kept her eyes closed. She couldn't sleep either. Had that text been from another woman? Debs, even? Maybe it was a money problem. They didn't have much, but they got by, didn't they? Or was he in debt? Maybe he was bored with her. She held back the tears. She loved him so much. She wanted to talk to him and find out the truth. But Linda was too frightened to ask.

CHAPTER EIGHTEEN

Friday, 10 February, 8.47 p.m.

Kevin closed the main doors of the bank, opened his briefcase and took out his small yellow B&Q torch. He used the shaft of light to take him through the darkness towards the security door and into his office.

He had kept his work clothes on for this evening, thinking that if he looked the part it wouldn't seem strange when he went into the bank at night. He had quite fancied wearing black overalls like de Niro did in *The Score*, but he'd thought they might look a bit odd on the bus home. Besides, he needed his briefcase to carry the contents of the safe-deposit box. An office suit and raincoat were more appropriate.

It had been easy getting into the bank. He had put his PIN number into the door alarm and left all the other alarms on. It wasn't as if he was going to attack the main vault, or blow his way in through a wall.

With the torch in his mouth Kevin knelt by his office safe and pulled the copy of Symington's key from his jacket pocket. He could hear shouts and thudding music from the two pubs further along the street. He had never been in this part of town so late at night. It was packed with young guys out for the night and most of them were pissed.

Slowly he turned the copy key and heard the clunk of the lock as it opened for him. He had done it! All he had to do now was open his own lock. He left the copy key in the safe lock, ready to secure it later. One of the lock picking websites had told Kevin that if a cut works first time, why take it out to maybe not work a second time?

With the torch in his mouth and dribble trickling down his chin, Kevin fished for the deposit-box guard key. He got up, picked up his briefcase and turned towards the door, lighting up the anniversary card and chocolates that Gary, Alice and Margaret had given him that morning. He had forgotten to take them home. It had been a nightmare trying to act as if today was like any other. Kevin had kept to his office as much as he could. He had been worried his face would give away his secret. He placed the card and chocolates in his briefcase and headed for the stairs.

Linda was at bingo with her mum and was never home until just after ten thirty. The bus to town had been twenty minutes late so he was cutting it fine. But he should still have enough time to get the bus home and be on the sofa watching *The Great Escape* when Linda came in.

At the bottom of the stairs, Kevin unlocked the door with his own key, opened it and pointed the torch at the wall of steel deposit-box doors on the other side of the room. A few more shouts came from the road, but they were soon cut off as Kevin closed the door behind him and turned on the light.

He was no longer thinking about what he was doing. He put the guard key into the deposit-box lock and turned. It opened with a gentle clunk. Kevin wasn't sure if it was excitement or fear that was making him feel a little light headed. He knelt in front of the boxes, opened his briefcase and pulled out his Dutch kit. It was an automatic lock pick that looked like an electronic screwdriver. But instead of a driver head sticking out the bottom there was a thin shaft of metal.

Kevin sat down with the instructions. He had spent many Friday nights reading instructions, usually for Ikea wardrobes, not 'How to Break into a Deposit Box'.

He put the two batteries into the

back of the pick and read on. It seemed simple enough. He switched it on, stood up and put it into the client lock. There was a gentle humming sound but the lock didn't budge. Kevin tried again. The lock opened. Success!

He stepped away from the box with the pick still in his hand. He turned it off, suddenly scared. This was it. He was going to rob the safe-deposit box. Kevin reached out and opened the steel door. It swung back with a gentle creak to reveal the black box. His fear left him.

He opened his briefcase, then reached inside the deposit box.

Suddenly, the bank's alarms ripped through the building. Fuck!

CHAPTER NINETEEN

Leaving the briefcase he ran up the stairs in blind panic. 'Shit! *Shit!*' He had to get away. He reached the top step with the alarm still in his ears, and ran to the main doors. There, he could hear police sirens above the alarm. His hands were shaking as he fumbled with the locks. The sirens were closer now. His fingers wouldn't work. He couldn't open the doors!

The sirens were outside now. Kevin fell against the door. Police radios crackled. He walked slowly back into the bank in a daze. All he could think of was Linda as blue lights flashed into his face. Suddenly he turned to the window. A wooden bench was sticking out through the smashed glass.

Kevin could see the police shouting at passers-by. But the alarm was too loud for him to make out what they were saying. Shit! What now?

He ran back downstairs to the safe-deposit box room. Closing the door behind him, he hit the lights.

He could still hear the alarms, but he felt safer in the darkness. The only other noise was the sound of his breathing. He leaned against the door, then slid to the floor, holding his head in his hands.

It was hopeless. He couldn't get film scenes of prison out of his mind and, worse, pictures of life without his Linda. He knew the police would surround the bank and the alarm company would already have called Symington. He started to cry. He wasn't a bank robber. He was a nobody.

His mobile was ringing. He hadn't even remembered to turn it off. He fumbled in his jacket pocket, grabbed at the phone. The display lit up. It was Symington. Could it get any worse?

The phone bleeped again. He still hadn't turned the fucking thing off. He listened to the message. Symington sounded as if he was in a pub. 'Where are you Dodds? I've left a message on your home number. There's been some vandalism at the bank. I'm going there now. Call me as soon as you get this.'

The system had swung into action and Kevin could not stop it. Symington would carry out his checks at the bank with a policeman. He would then report to Head Office. The glass people would arrive to patch up the window with plywood and in the morning they would replace the glass. The police would be outside all night, protecting the bank. It was then that Kevin started to tremble. The copy of the key was still in the safe lock!

The alarm fell silent. That meant Symington was in the bank. Kevin just sat and waited for the moment when his boss and the police would burst in and find him.

CHAPTER TWENTY

Kevin heard muffled voices upstairs. It wouldn't be long now. He wanted to see Linda, to cuddle her on the settee. Police radios were at the top of the stairs now. He racked his brains for what de Niro and Eastwood would do. For a start they wouldn't cry. And they wouldn't give up. Neither would he. Maybe the key wouldn't be noticed for a while. Maybe Symington would wait for him to turn up before he checked Kevin's office? Maybe. Maybe he had a few more minutes.

He wiped his face, switched on his torch, and quietly locked the door. If he was going to get nicked, he might as well get nicked red-handed. Fuck 'em. Kevin went back to the deposit box, reaching inside, he opened up the black box and quickly put its contents into his briefcase. Making sure he had also put the pick in his briefcase, he closed it before re-locking the deposit box. At least now he was a real bank robber.

Footsteps, more than one person, and the chatter of a police radio were coming down the stairs. Kevin gripped his briefcase and leaned back against the wall behind the door. He turned off the torch and held his breath. A key turned. The door swung open, with Kevin behind it. The light came on. Symington's face was inches away from his but on the other side of the door. 'All OK here. Although I'd like to know where my bloody deputy is.'

Just then Kevin's mobile vibrated in his hand.

The light was switched off and the door was locked again. He heard Symington and his escort go back upstairs.

Kevin looked down at the lit display. It was Linda. Shit! It was nearly ten! He kept his voice low.

'Hello?'

She was in the car. 'Where are you? I called home and I just got—'

'I'm at work. A bench has been thrown through the bank's window. I don't know when I'll get home. There's loads to do and—' Kevin could hear her crying. 'What's wrong? Your mum OK?'

'Fine. I've just dropped her off and I wanted to talk to you. I've been worried and when you didn't answer, well I . . . It's just I thought you'd left me.' She was sobbing now.

'Linda, stop the car, you'll have a crash.' Kevin forgot where he was and why. 'You parked up yet? Linda?'

There was no reply.

'Linda?'

'I thought you'd left, what with you staying up late online, the text last night, and then you not at home.' She was still sobbing. 'I was so worried. I thought you'd met someone else. You even started wearing hair gel.'

'Linda, it's OK. There isn't anyone else. I'll be home soon. Just calm down and take your time getting back. I'll be with you soon. I just have to finish here. OK?'

'I love you, Kevin.'

'I do too, sweetheart. I'll be home soon.'

CHAPTER TWENTY-ONE

He turned off the mobile. He needed time to think. There must a way out of this. There had to be. He couldn't be locked away in prison. He had to get home to his wife. He paced up and down in the darkness. He had to bluff his way out. After all, he did have a reason to be there. He was the deputy manager, and his boss had called him in. Kevin was muttering to himself as if he were getting a football team ready to go out on to the pitch. 'Come on now. Get a grip, Kev. You can do it.'

He took a deep breath, turned on the light and opened the door. As he did so, the noise from upstairs poured into the deposit-box room. He could hear glass smashing as the contractors cleared the glass out of the window frame. He had started to walk upstairs when he spotted a policeman at the top, looking down at him.

'Who are you?' the copper asked.

Kevin was too busy to look the man in the eye. He was checking his watch. 'The deputy manager. You know where the manager is?'

The policeman looked a little confused. 'How long have you been down there?'

Kevin walked past him, still without eye-contact. 'Far too long. Got lots more to do. You seen the manager?'

The policeman pointed towards Symington's office. Kevin walked through the bank, his shoes crunching over the glass on the floor. He went into his own office. The safe was still open. Had Symington seen it?

Kevin closed his office door. He dropped the briefcase on to his chair, then put the guard key back into the safe. He locked the safe and tucked the copy key into his jacket pocket. Then he covered his briefcase with his coat and headed for Symington's office. His boss was on the phone, talking to the Head Office duty manager. A theatre programme for *Lady Windermere's Fan* lay on his desk next to his overcoat. There was a photo of Jessica Drake on the front cover.

'He's here at last! Lucky I got in pretty quickly.'

Symington turned to Kevin. He liked to bollock him while Head Office was listening. 'I'm supposed to be able to contact you all the time, Dodds. Why couldn't I? You're supposed to be a professional.'

'Sorry, Mr Symington. I went straight from work to a friend's nearby and didn't get my messages. I didn't hear your call. I'm sorry. I—'

Symington had put up his hand to silence him. 'Let me get on with my work, Kevin, as you should be. Wait in your office for me to carry out a deposit-box key check.' Then Symington spoke into the phone. 'No, I haven't checked the CCTV tapes yet. Just the vault and deposit boxes. I'll look at them now.'

Kevin went into his office, hardly daring to breathe. All he had to do was keep his cool, and he'd soon be able to get out of there. He switched on his mobile, and tried to keep his voice steady. 'Hello, darling. I'm going to be a couple more hours yet, so don't wait up. And I'm really sorry, but I'll probably have to come into work in the morning. Head Office security visit.'

Kevin could hear banging from the

next-door office. Symington was going mad. 'Where are those bloody tapes!'

Even Linda could hear him. 'I understand. Who was that, Kevin?'

'Just Symington doing the usual. I'll see you soon, darling. I can't wait for tomorrow night.'

He switched off the phone. If he'd had one of Clint's cigars right then, he would have lit it.

CHAPTER TWENTY-TWO

Saturday, 11 Febuary, 8.20 p.m.

Kevin parked the car, then he and Linda crossed the road to Marco's. Linda was still questioning him about last night. Kevin had been forced to spend the best part of the afternoon at the bank, talking to Head Office and filling in forms. 'Will Symington really get the sack for not getting videos of those yobs?'

'They'll make him take early retirement. It's funny, but I feel a bit sorry for him. Anyway, he'll get a big fat pension. The bank needs to keep him happy. They won't want their customers to find out that they let the world's worst bank manger look after their money for so long.'

'Do you really think you might get the job?' she whispered, as if it felt too risky to say it out loud. 'Tell me *exactly* what he said again.' She wanted yet another blow-by-blow account of what the general manager had told him.

' "Let's book a meeting on Monday for you to come up to Head Office. We'll discuss your future and the branch's long-overdue refit." '

Linda kissed his cheek, excited, as Kevin pushed open the door for her. He followed his wife in. The restaurant was packed, everyone enjoying their Saturday night out. As Linda took off her coat and hung it over the back of her chair, Kevin saw again how beautiful she was. Her freshly blow-dried hair swung across her face as she sat down.

'Good evening, Mr and Mrs Dodds. A pleasure to see you again.' Mark placed two glasses of champagne on their table. 'Please accept these on the house, and may I congratulate you on your wedding anniversary. I hope you have a lovely evening.' He lit the candle on their table and left them alone to look at menus.

Something caught Kevin's eye at the far end of the room. 'Bloody hell! That's Dave from school—over there. He's punky Debs's husband. But that's not her with him.'

Linda turned to see Dave with a young blonde girl. Her hand was in his on the table, and they were gazing into each other's eyes. 'Yuk! I almost feel sorry for Debs.'

Kevin thought back to the way she'd taken the piss out of him and

Linda on the bus but couldn't help feeling the same. 'Me too. But let's forget about them and tonight just think about us.' He lifted his champagne glass, 'To our happy marriage and lots more happy years to come.'

'To our happy marriage.' They clinked glasses.

Linda picked up her handbag. 'Now it's present time. Close your eyes and open your hands.' Kevin opened his arms as wide as if he was about to carry a tree-trunk. 'Smaller.' He moved his hands a few inches in. 'Smaller.' His palms were touching when he felt something laid in them.

He opened his eyes, tore open the envelope and two flight tickets fell out on to the table. 'What's this?' He already knew the answer.

His smile grew wider as Linda rattled off the details. 'Our five-star Greek holiday! Just think, Kev! Sun, sea and sand. I've been saving up for the last year. No caravan for us!'

He leaned across the table, pulled her head towards him and kissed her lips. He didn't care who saw him. 'Thank you, sweetheart. It's the best present ever. I can't wait.' Kevin reached into his inside pocket. 'And now for yours. Close your eyes and open your hands.' Linda cupped her hands and brought them in front of her.

He dropped the slim black box into them.

Linda smiled as she wrapped her fingers round the leather and opened her eyes. 'Mmm. Looks good already.' She snapped the box open and her jaw dropped. She was silent for a moment, but her eyes said it all.

'The Augusta!' It was the loudest whisper anyone had ever heard. Now it was Kevin's turn to grin from ear to ear.

'I just love it, Kevin. You know I do. Thank you so so much. I bet it cost a fortune and this one looks amazing. Look how the pearls glow.

You'd never know. They're so beautiful. Thank you.'

She took the necklace out of its box and put the Augusta round her neck. As the diamonds sparkled in the candle-light, his wife had never been more beautiful. She was a princess.

'Thank you, Kevin. I don't care if we're broke for the rest of our lives. I love my Augusta, and I love you.'

Kevin couldn't contain his excitement. He also felt guilty. 'Linda, I need to tell you the truth about all that extra work I've been doing this week, and what I did last night.'

Linda was still smiling, not really taking it all in.

Kevin leaned over the table to whisper, 'I robbed the bank. My bank. And it was great.'

'Yeah, yeah, yeah. Got old Rowland's money, did you? Are we off to buy our island?' She stroked the necklace. 'And are you going to buy the real one now?'

'Linda. It *is* the real one . . .' He told her the whole story, how he switched Linda's Augusta with the real one in Jessica Drake's deposit box.

'Course you did, Kev,' she said, when he'd finished. 'I'd expect no less of you on our anniversary.' She smiled. 'Listen, I don't care that this Augusta isn't real.'

'But it is. I've got to go back to the deposit box tomorrow night and swap it back again. She's leaving town on Monday.'

'You don't need to pretend it's the real one, darling. It's beautiful, and you gave it to me, so it's even more special than Jessica Drake's. You're the best husband in the world, Kevin Dodds.' She picked up her glass. 'I propose a toast to my perfect husband.'

Just then two guitarists in red shirts appeared, strolled up to their table and started to play.

Kevin raised his glass to his wife. The musicians were playing a Billy Joel song. *Their* Billy Joel song. Just as Kevin had asked Mark to arrange. ' "I love you just the way you are", Linda. I want to tell you over and over again. I love you. I love you. I love you.' Linda was overwhelmed. As the guitarists played on, her eyes filled with tears.

Tears welled in Kevin's eyes too. Everything felt different now, and really good. It was the biggest kick in the world to see his beautiful wife wearing a priceless necklace. He hadn't wanted to rob the bank for money, it wasn't about that. And it didn't matter that nobody knew what he had done. What mattered was that *he* knew, and he was proud of himself. Never again would he let women like Debs take the piss out of him or his wife. Never again would he be pushed around by the Symingtons and Jessica Drakes of this world. The grey man had gone.

Kevin drank the last of his champagne. 'You know what, Linda?' She looked up from her Augusta and smiled.

'Change of plan. I'm not going back to the bank tomorrow night. You keep the real one. You deserve it.'